Merry Christmas, Splat

Merry Christmas, Nicky, Donna, and Frankie
—R.S.

Special thanks to Maria.

ISBN 978-0-545-27976-5

12 11 10 9 8   13 14 15/0

Printed in the U.S.A.   40

First Scholastic printing, September 2010

Typography by Jeanne L. Hogle

Rob Scotton

Merry Christmas, Splat

SCHOLASTIC INC.
New York Toronto London Auckland
Sydney Mexico City New Delhi Hong Kong

"It's very important to write a letter to Santa," said Splat. "How else will he know what to bring you for Christmas?" Seymour nodded.

Splat's pencil scratched across the page until . . .
"Finished!" he exclaimed, and proudly showed off his lette
Seymour was impressed.
Splat's little sister wasn't.

Dear Santa,
Can I please have a
really big present for
Christmas?
Thank you, Splat
ps i have been a very good cat

"Only good cats get really big presents from Santa," she said.
"Are you sure you've been good?"
"Of course," said Splat.
She gave Splat a look that only little sisters can give.

"R-e-a-l-l-y?"

Splat stuck his nose in the air and marched out of the kitchen.

"I have been good," he said.
Seymour nodded.

"In fact, I've been very good."
This time Seymour shrugged, and Splat had an
awful thought that made his tail quiver and twitch.

Maybe I haven't been good enough.

Splat tried hard to remember.

"Yes!" he decided. "I'm sure I have . . .
but just in case—"

"MOM!" cried Splat. "I'm going to help you
get everything ready for Christmas!"

"Oh dear," said his mom.
Splat took that to mean "Thank
you very much. You really
are a good little cat."
And he set about being
ever so helpful.

"I've washed the Christmas dishes, Mom," said Splat.
"Thank you, Splat," said his mom. "But the dishes weren't dirty."

"I know," replied Splat. "And still I washed them!
I'm just so good."

"The Christmas tree is decorated now, Mom," Splat called.
"I thought it was already done," replied his mom.
"Not even close," said Splat. "But it is now."

"I'm going to clear the snow from the path, Mom," said Splat.
"Wait!" his mom called.

"Don't . . . open . . . the door."

"Being so good is very tiring," said Splat.
"It certainly is," said his mom.

"I think I'll go to bed now,"
Splat announced.

"Good idea," said his mom.

Splat snuggled under the covers and closed his eyes.
But his eyes wouldn't stay closed.
*Maybe I'd better wait up for Santa and tell him how good
I've been,* thought Splat.

So Splat took his flashlight from the drawer and waited.

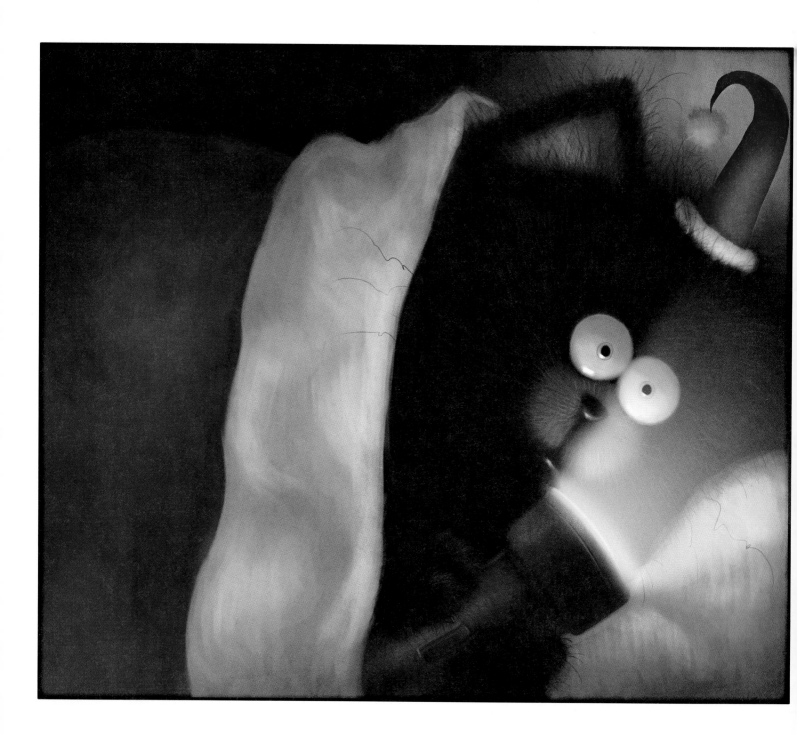

All was quiet . . . until *clip-clop, clip-clop.*
Splat heard reindeer on the roof!

But the *clip-clop* slowly turned to *tick-tock*.

It was only his clock.

Splat rolled over just in time to see a shadow appear on the wall.

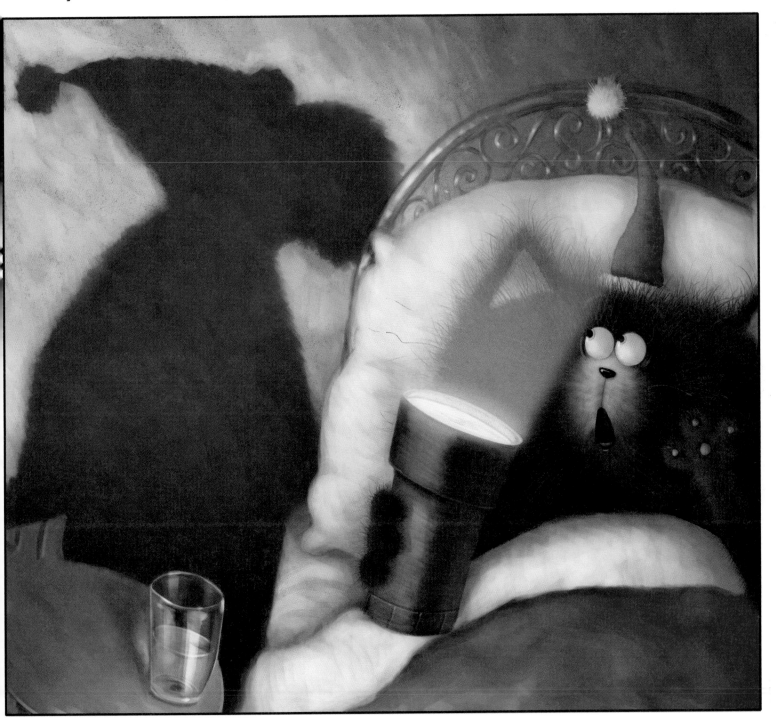

"Santa!" Splat called.

But it was only Seymour making an ice angel on the window.

Splat huffed, plumped up his pillow,
and waited some more.

Santa has to come soon, thought Splat.

But the rest of the night passed silently . . .

peacefully . . . with not even a whisper.

Christmas morning shone through Splat's bedroom
window, but he was not the least bit excited.
His little sister came in to wake him.
"I guess I haven't been good enough after all," said Splat.

"Told you so," said his little sister. "But you can play with Kitty if you like."

"Thanks . . ." Splat said in a little voice.

Splat's little sister led him down the stairs.
It was too quiet.

There were no presents around the tree, and the
rest of his family was nowhere to be seen.
"Because I haven't been good enough," said Splat,
"Santa hasn't visited us at all."

But then Splat's family leaped out from behind the sofa.

"MERRY CHRISTMAS, SPLAT," they cheered.

And they were holding a really big present.
Just for Splat.

"It's the best Christmas present ever!" cried Splat.